READING CHAMPION

Where Are We Going?

by **Elizabeth Dale** and **Amanda Gulliver**

FRANKLIN WATTS
LONDON•SYDNEY

Max and Ann went on a train.
Mum went, too.

"Where are we going?"
said Max.

They saw a pond.

"Can we feed the ducks?"
said Ann.
"Can we get off?"

But the train went on.

They saw a fun fair.

"Can we go on the slide?"
said Max.
"Can we get off?"

But the train went on.

They saw a park.

"Can we go in the sand?"
said Ann.
"Can we get off?"

But the train went on.

They saw a river.

"Can we go in the water?"
said Max.
"Can we get off?"

But the train went on.

11

They saw the beach.

"Can we go to the beach?"
said Ann and Max.

"Yes," said Mum.
"We can go to the beach."

"We can feed the ducks,"
said Ann.

"We can go on the slide, too,"
said Max.

15

"We can go in the water,"
said Max.

"We can play in the sand, too,"
said Mum.

17

Max and Ann had fun
at the beach.

Mum did, too.

Story trail

Start

Start at the beginning of the story trail. Ask your child to retell the story in their own words, pointing to each picture in turn to recall the sequence of events.

Independent Reading

This series is designed to provide an opportunity for your child to read on their own. These notes are written for you to help your child choose a book and to read it independently.

In school, your child's teacher will often be using reading books which have been banded to support the process of learning to read. Use the book band colour your child is reading in school to help you make a good choice. *Where Are We Going?* is a good choice for children reading at Yellow Band in their classroom to read independently.

The aim of independent reading is to read this book with ease, so that your child enjoys the story and relates it to their own experiences.

About the book

Max and Ann are on the train with Mum. They look out of the window and see lots of fun things to do. They want to get off and join in, but the train goes on. Luckily, when they arrive at the beach, they can do all the things they wanted to do.

Before reading

Help your child to learn how to make good choices by asking: "Why did you choose this book? Why do you think you will enjoy it?" Look at the cover together and ask: "What do you think the story will be about?" Support your child to think of what they already know about the story context. Read the title aloud and ask: "Why are they asking where they are going? Who do you think is asking this question?" Remind your child that they can try to sound out the letters to make a word if they get stuck.

Decide together whether your child will read the story independently or read it aloud to you. When books are short, as at Yellow Band, your child may wish to do both!

During reading

If reading aloud, support your child if they hesitate or ask for help by telling the word. Remind your child of what they know and what they can do independently.

If reading to themselves, remind your child that they can come and ask for your help if stuck.

After reading

Support comprehension by asking your child to tell you about the story. Help your child think about the messages in the book that go beyond the story and ask: "Do you think that Max and Ann are happy that they ended up at the beach? Why/why not"

Give your child a chance to respond to the story: "Did you have a favourite part? Where would you like to go for a day out?"

Use the story trail to encourage your child to retell the story in the right sequence, in their own words.

Extending learning

Help your child understand the story structure by using the same sentence patterns and adding some new elements. "Let's make up a new story about Max and Ann going somewhere else. In my story they are on a journey to visit the nature park. They saw a playground. 'Look! Can we go on the swings?' said Ann. 'Can we get off?' But the train went on. They saw a stream. 'Look! Can we cross on the stepping stones?' said Max. 'Can we get off?' But the train went on. Now you try. Where will Max and Ann go in your story?"

Your child's teacher will be talking about punctuation at Yellow Band. On a few of the pages, check your child can recognise capital letters, full stops and question marks by asking them to point these out.

Franklin Watts
First published in Great Britain in 2017
by The Watts Publishing Group

Copyright © The Watts Publishing Group 2017

Series Editors: Jackie Hamley and Melanie Palmer
Series Advisors: Dr Sue Bodman and Glen Franklin
Series Designer: Peter Scoulding

A CIP catalogue record for this book is
available from the British Library.

ISBN 978 1 4451 5473 2 (hbk)
ISBN 978 1 4451 5474 9 (pbk)
ISBN 978 1 4451 6081 8 (library ebook)

Printed in China

Franklin Watts
An imprint of
Hachette Children's Group
Part of The Watts Publishing Group
Carmelite House
50 Victoria Embankment
London EC4Y 0DZ

An Hachette UK Company
www.hachette.co.uk

www.franklinwatts.co.uk